About the author

Mo lives in London. Born an Aries, with boundless energy and a curiosity for anything and everything, she loves riding her FJ motorcycle. She is passionate about the welfare and wellbeing of animals and is a vegan. She has a son and a daughter, and is a grandmother and great grandmother.

A SLICE OF LIFE

Mo Tritton

A SLICE OF LIFE

Vanguard Press

VANGUARD PAPERBACK

© Copyright 2020
Mo Tritton

The right of Mo Tritton to be identified as author of
this work has been asserted by her in accordance with the
Copyright, Designs and Patents Act 1988.

All Rights Reserved

No reproduction, copy or transmission of this publication
may be made without written permission.
No paragraph of this publication may be reproduced,
copied or transmitted save with the written permission of the
publisher, or in accordance with the provisions
of the Copyright Act 1956 (as amended).

Any person who commits any unauthorised act in relation to
this publication may be liable to criminal
prosecution and civil claims for damages.

A CIP catalogue record for this title is
available from the British Library.

ISBN 9781784656 60-7

Vanguard Press is an imprint of
Pegasus Elliot MacKenzie Publishers Ltd.
www.pegasuspublishers.com

First Published in 2020

Vanguard Press
Sheraton House Castle Park
Cambridge England

Printed & Bound in Great Britain

Dedication

This book is dedicated to the absolute magic of all Life on Earth and the fragility of each moment.

Prologue

He couldn't move, trapped as he was in a tiny metal cage, the bars pressing into him making parts of his clothing squeeze out between some of the bars, his head bent low, chin pressing into his chest trying desperately to breathe as his knees pressed into his face. He could only take shallow breaths, his chest could not expand any further. He tried his best not to panic but suddenly let out a scream of fear as the cage he was in was moved. A heavy iron bar hit the side of the cage making an awful noise in that confined space that threatened to pierce his eardrums followed by 'Shadup' from one of the men outside manoeuvring the cage towards the edge of the pier. He couldn't see the outside of the cage with his head in the position it was but he began to plead for his life. The cage finally toppled off of the pier and ungracefully dived into the waiting sea sinking without hesitation. He was drowning, coughing and spluttering, trying desperately to hold onto the last precious mouthful of oxygen. The bubbles of life floated up and away as he swiftly raced to the bottom of the sea.

    Harry woke with a gasp, sweat pouring off of him. It was a dream, only a dream, thank goodness. His heart was pounding in his chest as he sat up in bed and looked around the room to try to anchor himself. He swung his legs over the edge of the bed and stood up, swaying slightly from the dregs of the dream, 'coffee' he thought as he moved towards the kitchenette, barely big enough to stand in, let alone, cook in. 'Still, musn't grumble' he thought stopping briefly at the hall mirror to look at himself and grimacing at the sight of himself. He could do with a good nights' sleep that's for sure and oh how he wished he could have one, every night seemed to outdo itself in dredging up frightmares these days.

The coffee made him feel so much better so he made a second cup whilst running his bath then gratefully got into it, his coffee balanced at one end of the bath whilst his sweat soaked pyjamas curled up on the floor like a wet cat. He had a half smile on his face as he recognised the irony of getting into water after such an appalling dream, still, it was only a dream. Another one to add to a long list of bad dreams, he should be getting used to them by now. The warm soapy water worked its magic on him and he finally began to relax as cosy thoughts cuddled his brain enveloping him comfort.

***

1987

They were going to the seaside, they were actually going to the seaside. Harry was full up to the top of himself with excitement, in fact he was overfull and his excitement had him rushing about as fast as he could helping out but in reality, slowing down the preparations that were taking place. His shrill little voice constantly questioned either parent to get reassurance that they were actually going to the coast.

Harry unpacked his bag his mother had packed for him just to check what was inside it but couldn't get the contents back in it.

Finally, they were ready to leave and had just closed the front door behind them when Harry remembered Johnny bunny, he couldn't possibly go without him. His mother said that Johnny bunny was looking after the house for them but in the end Johnny bunny went with them, one of his little paws was tightly held by Harry, his feet trailing on the ground. There was a label sewn inside his coat, 'This bunny belongs to…' with the address just in case he ever got mislaid or separated from Harry. Harry loved him.

It was a lovely day, the sun smiling down on them plus a gentle breeze to ruffle their hair. They waited at the bus stop for quite a long time but eventually their bus came and they settled themselves in their seats with Harry telling everybody on board that they were going to the seaside, his big blue eyes and brown curly hair and obvious excitement enchanting everybody.

Harry let go of his Dads' hand whilst he bought the tickets for the journey then quickly grabbed it again as they went up onto the platform. They didn't have to wait long and soon they were settled on seats side by side as the train took them into the city.

Harry felt very important sitting on a seat by himself his legs stretched out straight in front of him, his bag and Johnny bunny on his lap. He thought the train was very noisy and wasn't too sure if he liked being on it or not. Before too long, however, they disembarked into a very busy station. Harry held tight onto his Dads' hand, all he could see of the world were endless legs, dogs on leads and occasional pushchairs. The platform was crowded, there were so many people. Harry wondered if they were all going to the seaside!

They soon boarded another train and found seats opposite each other that they could relax in. Harry was thrilled to be sitting by the window and watching the town and countryside slip past. He huffed on the window and drew patterns in it but before long his eyes began to droop and he fell fast asleep. His Dad pulled him back onto the seat and put an arm around him to stop him slipping off of the seat. As Harry relaxed

Johnny bunny slipped from his grasp onto the floor of the train.

His Dad shook him awake "Come on son, we're here" and helped Harry off of the train with Mum descending behind. Still sleepy, Harry held on to his Dads' hand as the family threaded through the crowds and out of the station. Harry was lifted up onto his Dads' shoulders so that he could have a brilliant view of the surroundings. There was almost too much to take in, the pavements full of people jostling each other, noisy open-fronted arcades full of machines spewing out numbers, patterns or ditties, and ice cream vendors selling ices of different flavours, colours and toppings, whilst overhead the shrill cries of seagulls as they floated effortlessly in the sky above.

Harry was wide awake now and wriggled so much in excitement that his Dad had to lift him off of his shoulders and put him back down on the ground in case he fell.

The atmosphere was electric. Harry chatted away and was only finally silenced for a few minutes or so by having a huge stick of candy floss bought for him.

It was quite a long walk down the High Street to the beach but finally they arrived on the promenade. The beach sloped down to the high tide mark, depicted by stones, shells and brown seaweed, that stretched away as far as the eye could see. They chose a place on the beach and whilst his Dad went off to rent some deckchairs Harry unpacked his bag and settled down to make sandcastles.

Harry laughed when his Dad clowned around putting up the deckchairs but soon the family were settled. Harry changed into some swimming shorts then his Mum made him stand still whilst she rubbed sun lotion over him. Finally, he settled down to play in the sand whilst his Mum got out some knitting and his Dad opened a newspaper.

Harry buried his bag in the sand and asked his Mum to help him find it. She looked everywhere except where it was, with Harry giggling at her efforts until he finally 'found it' and held it up triumphantly. She tickled him and he rolled around in the sand laughing joyously then she went back to her knitting reminding him not to move too far away from them.

He had a great time building then knocking down sandcastles, covering his legs with sand then writing his name in the sand. He looked over at his parents and realised they were asleep. He watched them for a little while then carried on playing with the sand. The children of a family nearby were carrying buckets of water up to their sandcastle and were obviously having a lot of fun splashing it down into the moat they had made. Harry looked down towards the sea and was surprised to see that the tide had come in already. He got up to go down to it then stopped and turned back towards his parents, "I'm just going down there" he pointed to the sea "to get some water in my bucket" and he walked down to the water's edge. The water was warm and the waves tickled his feet. Harry stamped his feet up and down making little splashes, with a grin on his face that stretched from ear to ear. He sat down and watched as the waves rolled over his legs then drew away. After a time, he remembered he had only come down to fill his bucket with water so he filled it then poured the water over himself.

"Hallo young man" a voice interrupted his concentration and he looked up to see a person he did not know. Harry made as if to get up but stopped as the person continued with "That looks fun can you show me how to do it?"

Harry sat down again and said, "You do this," filling the bucket with water, "then you do this, see," as he poured the water over his legs.

"That's clever," the person said and Harry puffed up with pride and repeated the actions a few more times. When offered an ice cream Harry immediately stopped what he was doing and stood up and held the hand that was offered out to him and was about to follow when he heard his name called loudly and looking up the beach, he saw his Dad waving at him. Ice cream forgotten he let go of the persons hand and scrambled up the beach shouting "Daddy, Daddy." He found trying to run uphill through the soft sand heavy going and it wasn't too long before he went flying face down into it, his bucket soaring off to the side. His Dad pulled him upright onto his feet and dusted him down at the same time visually checking he was not hurt whilst verbally asking him the same thing. When reassured Harry was not hurt, he knelt down in front of him and put his hands onto his shoulders asking him why he had moved so far away from them and who was that person he had been with? Harry told him that they were going to buy an ice cream whilst waving his arm and pointing back in the direction he had come from. His Dad stood up and scoured the beach looking for the person he had seen nearby Harry but there was no sign of him. Harry took his Dads' hand and went back up the beach to where the deckchairs were chatting away about getting an ice cream. His parents spent the next few minutes reminding Harry of the dangers of talking to and walking away with strangers, their worried faces causing him to burst into tears. He was frightened because his parents were frightened but had no real idea of the danger he might have put himself in.

His Mum began sorting out the packed lunches she had made for them and soon he was unpacking his lunch with excitement, he felt really grown up.

Later that day the family walked along the pier and stood at the end of it enjoying the cooling sea breezes whilst in tune with the endless motion of the sea.

The walk back up the High Street seemed longer than the walk down in the morning and they were glad to reach the station and board the train on their return journey. Harry fell asleep almost as soon as he sat down and in fact didn't remember much about the return journey at all, but he did realise that Johnny Bunny was missing when he went to bed that evening and reached for him. He was inconsolable for many hours and finally fell asleep exhausted, tucked in between his parents. As for Johnny bunny he was none the worse the wear for his adventure, but returned home via the Post Office full of exciting adventures to tell Harry.

***

2019

It was the cold water more than the daydreaming that brought him wide awake. After getting dressed he put his meagre possessions in his battered, brown suitcase, did a quick check around the room, making sure it was as clean and tidy as he had first found it, then went downstairs leaving the bedroom keys on the hall table as requested. As Harry walked along the High Street towards the train station he reflected on his stay. He'd been in this part of town for nearly two weeks, two weeks, he couldn't believe it, it was the longest he had stayed anywhere for a long time. He was becoming comfortable with the area and the people who lived there and that was the problem for him, the minute you relax your guard, your emotions come into play, making you vulnerable. Harry didn't want that, he didn't want to give someone the opportunity of getting to know him, of building relationships, of falling in love and getting hurt. No way. He stopped inside a small café and ordered a late breakfast. He sat down by the steamy windows with a large mug of tea whilst he waited for his order and stared into it as he stirred it round and round and round.

***

1989

Harry came in from school to the delicious smell of home baking. He shrugged out of his school blazer, kicked his shoes into the cupboard under the stairs and slung his satchel on the sofa then went into the kitchen. His Mum had the radio on and was singing along with it as she mixed and whisked ingredients. He loved cooking and often helped in making cakes and cooking dinners. He could toss a pancake better than anyone, so he said, and he was certainly better at doing it than his parents. Helping himself to biscuits from the tin and a drink from the fridge, he went into the larder and took some fresh greens and carrots for his pet rabbit Misty and her companion, a ginger guinea pig called Gloria.

In the middle of the garden was a pond that he had helped his Dad to build many years ago. When they had finished building it the pond looked enormous to Harry but now, as he knelt by it, it looked really small. He saw some water boatmen on it and watched as insects came down to the edge to drink. Harry had always worried about small creatures drowning in it so he made sure that pieces of twigs and branches were in it so that anything unfortunate enough to fall in could get out. He had a half smile on his face as he remembered searching for round smooth stones to place around the pond and showing his Dad each one that he had found.

    Harry continued down the garden going around the side of the shed to where the hutch and run were. He heard Gloria chirruping away long before he saw her making a nest in a huge pile of torn paper. Misty was out in the run busily washing a stretched out back leg. He put the fresh vegetables in the food dish after taking out the uneaten ones from yesterday. Misty briefly stopped washing her leg to watch him then started licking the inside of both paws and washing her face, she looked so cute doing this and Harry stayed watching her then refreshed the water bottles and returned down the garden. He sat at the dining table doing his homework to get it out of the way then made himself an omelette for his tea before going up to his room.

***

2019

The breakfast being plonked down in front of him brought Harry back from his daydreaming, he asked for another mug of tea as the previous one had grown cold and tucked in to his breakfast.

Walking down the High Street soon after Harry made his way to the station without being drawn in to the festive displays in the windows of the shops he passed. It is doubtful whether he even realised that the festive season was fast approaching having become an expert at withdrawing himself from life in general. He had become a nomad, no roots, no ties and almost no feelings, except when they caught him unawares and spilled over into his life or dreams. Harry did not know how to deal with emotions so he bottled them up as best he could and kept on the move.

This way of life had worked for him for many years and he saw no reason to change it. Harry did not see it as avoiding facing up to things, he called himself a free spirit that was blown where ever the wind would take him.

Once on the train he settled in a window seat and watched the world fly by.

***

1992

Harry was the class comedian, jokes rolled off of his tongue thick and fast. Always getting into trouble for talking he was the sort of child that had charisma. He loved science and anything to do with water (apart from washing) and always got top marks in this subject. During one lesson they learnt how to float a needle on top of water and Harry was made up about this and decided to put on a show for his parents.

Later that same evening he got his parents to sit on the settee and made them a cup of tea whilst he prepared himself. He had already prepared a small fish tank with water and covered it with a cloth and had placed a large sewing needle that he had borrowed from his Mum beside it, now all he had to do was to get himself ready.

Harry pulled the sleeves of his coat through to the wrong side to make a cape then made a cone out of some newspaper found in the bottom of the hall cupboard. He knew how to do this as his Dad had shown him when they were looking for something to hold popcorn in. Harry then gave himself a moustache with boot polish then made his entrance into the front room. The door burst open and Harry threw his arms wide, "Tada, I am Omo the…" but didn't get to finish the sentence as the minute he threw his arms wide his cloak fell off then as he bent down to retrieve it his hat fell off and the door swung back and knocked him on the head. His mum and dad thought it was amazing and laughed and clapped until Harry pointed out that he hadn't started yet.

Harry unveiled the tank of water and showed his parents the needle that he would float on water then asked them to shut their eyes tight and imagine the needle was floating.

Two minutes later Harry asked them to open their eyes and to their astonishment they saw the needle floating on top of the water. They clapped and cheered, Harry bowed and returned his coat into the hall cupboard, his paper hat onto the pile of newspapers then went upstairs into the bathroom to wash the boot polish off of his face but even after rubbing and scrubbing vigorously he still was left with a faint impression of a moustache. Hopefully it would have disappeared by the time he went to school on Monday or he was in for some ribbing from his mates.

***

2019

The train on which Harry was travelling was held up for some reason not that he was too concerned about it. Life in all its many wondrous forms was happening all around him but he refused to be part of it, navigating around it's edges suited him fine.

The carriage was full with some restless children running up and down the centre aisle whilst their mother attempted to placate a teething baby. One of the children came a cropper and began to wail loudly. Their mother looked around, saw Harry watching, said, "Do you mind," and put the baby on his lap whilst she went to tend to her wailing child. The baby stopped grizzling and looked up into Harry's face whilst gnawing on her fingers with her gums then pointing with a finger to where her mother was saying, "Dad, Dad, Dad." Harry was captivated at this valiant attempt to communicate and found himself smiling down at her and was rewarded by a big beaming smile. It wasn't until the Mother had lifted the baby back off of his lap and said, "Thank you so much," that he missed the warmth and weight of the little one. He got up and moved to another part of the train quickly receding into his shell.

The station he disembarked at was very busy and Harry had to queue to get through the turnstiles. Once out of the station he turned the opposite way to which the majority of pedestrians were going and clutching his battered brown suitcase strolled along the road as if he knew where he was going. Harry decided to find himself some lodgings after he had had something to eat and before long came across a public house The Swalk' with a 'homemade food all day' sign chalked outside it and went inside and ordered a meal and a pint.

As Harry tucked into his meal his mind ambled back to the baby sitting on his lap and smiling up at him. Despite his unwillingness to interact with other people a thought suddenly popped into his head as to what it would be like to have a child or children of his own. What would they look like, what would they grow up to be! 'Woops' he thought, 'I'm getting a bit ahead of myself here, I'm in danger of re-joining the human race if I am not careful.' The thoughts sat nicely with him though and, for the first time in his life he wondered what it would be like to settle down somewhere with a bit of land, somewhere where he could rediscover himself and actually live his life with a family surrounding him and getting a dog or dogs and also turkeys and chickens free ranging instead of leading a lonely nomadic existence. He was lonely, but that was down to him and now, perhaps, it was time for him to change things.

Something within him was stirring and he opened himself up to it.

***

1995

His parents wanted him to go shopping with them but it was the last thing he wanted. He loved his parents but to be actually seen out with them, uggh. However, choice was taken from him and later that same day found the family of three getting off of the bus, crossing the road and walking under the railway arch to the shopping complex.

It was a very well thought out complex with a wide variety of shops that attracted a lot of people from outside the borough. Harry was caught up in the hustle and bustle and became a very enthusiastic window shopper, especially when he discovered gadget shops.

The family finally reached the top floor of the complex via the escalators and went into a well-known bicycle shop. Harry wandered around the shop whilst his parents chatted to a sales person, seeing if the bells or the bicycle pumps worked. He looked over at his parents and saw his Dad watching him with a frown on his face. Harry put on an innocent expression as well as putting his hands in his pockets so as not to touch anything else. His Dad nodded at him then turned his attention back to the salesperson. Harry continued to wander around the shop and suddenly stopped and stared, before him was a beautiful red bicycle with thick off-road tyres, beautiful. It didn't cost anything to look at it he thought and looking around to see if anyone was nearby, he took hold of the handlebar and swung his leg over the frame.

"Found something you like then," his Dad said walking towards him with his Mum slightly behind him talking to the salesperson walking beside her.

Harry got off of the bike and nodded at his Dad who then looked behind him at his wife and nodded at her. She then walked off with the salesperson whilst his Dad looked the bike over then clapped Harry on his shoulder "Early birthday present son," he said and laughed as Harrys' mouth fell open. Actually, his birthday was just a few days away but Harry had ascended to cloud nine when his Dad had said those magic words and tingled with excitement.

"No, you're kidding me. No, not really, is it really. I don't believe it, I love it." Harry threw his arms around his Dad and hugged him so tightly burying his head in his Dads' chest. His Mum came over to them and the three of them love hugged.

"It will be delivered on your birthday," said his smiling Mum. Harry wanted to take it with them now although it wasn't really practical but Mum said the delivery arrangements had been made and he would just have to wait a few days.

Harry knew of the sacrifices that had been made by his parents in order to buy him the bike. He suddenly turned and looked back at them as they walked hand in hand smiling at each other.

"Thank you, thank you, thank you ever so much," he said. He was so full of emotion he wanted to jump up and touch the moon, the smile on his face stretching from ear to ear.

The family left the shopping arcade and walked under the railway bridge then turned left towards the bus stop which was about twenty yards away. There were a few shops just passed the railway bridge, the nearest one being a small jewellery shop in which his parents had first purchased their engagement then wedding rings. They stopped, still hand in hand, in front of the window as Harry continued on to the bus stop, having no interest in the jewellery shop whatsoever or being seen with lovey dovey parents. Reaching the bus stop he checked down the road to see if a bus was coming then, looping one arm around the stop swung around it as he usually did. As he swung around for the second time, he saw a 4 x 4 mounting the pavement and aiming straight for the jewellery store. His grip slipped from the bus stop causing him to fall down at the same time as a strangled warning to his parents tried to escape from his mouth but never made it. Everything seemed to be in slow motion as he watched the 4 x 4 stalk his parents, who were blissfully unaware of the tragedy unfolding behind them as they window shopped, still holding hands and pointing at various items in the window.

They never had a chance of course and it is doubtful whether they were ever aware or even heard the strangled cry that eventually managed to escape Harrys' mouth before they were mown down.

The 4 x 4 completely smashed the front of the shop coming to a standstill inside it.

Silence ensued briefly.

Harry screamed his parents' names then ran towards the shop but was held back by a couple of people. He struggled to get away from them, and almost did a couple of times but eventually sank to the ground still screaming and calling out to his parents.

Luckily there had been no customers or staff in the front of the shop now occupied by the 4 x 4, so apart from the shock of what had actually happened and the shock from what might have happened to them if they had been serving there were no other victims than Mr and Mrs Smith.

The driver, having suffered a mild stroke was, at this time, still in the vehicle slumped over the steering wheel. Due to being unconscious he didn't hear the bodywork of his vehicle complaining of its injuries as it began to cool and settle in the shop front.

The police, fire brigade and an ambulance duly arrived and the area around the shop was cordoned off.

Harry remembered being treated for shock by some paramedics but very little else. He didn't know if he was given something for shock or if he just succumbed to sleep, but he was thankful to escape the turmoil in his mind.

He awoke in a strange room having no idea who he was, where he was or what time it was. He threw back the duvet and looked out of the window at an ordinary street full of parked cars and people. Harry knew there was something very important that he had to remember but what it was eluded him.

Once in the bathroom he stared at his reflection but was unable to put a name to the person he saw. He turned away and, coming out of the bathroom, bumped into a woman he had never seen before.

"Nice to see you are finally awake, if you want breakfast, I can do you some," she said to him but Harry simply stared at her then tried to move around her. "Come down when you are ready," she spoke to him once more as she went downstairs, "by the way my name is Rosey."

Harry sat on his bed for a moment confused then memories of the previous day hurled themselves at him and he buried himself beneath the duvet sobbing, his body racked with the pain of loss.

***

2019

Harry thoroughly enjoyed his meal and after ordering another pint he went out into the garden to drink it. Just beyond the garden wall was moorland stretching as far as the eye could see, wild and beautiful. It did his heart good to see it, as yet unspoilt.

Leaving the public house Harry crossed over the road and turned into a neat tree-line suburban street. He passed a few B & B rooms available signs before he stopped at one, random selection, and knocked at the door.

There was no immediate answer and Harry was just turning away when he noticed the bell with the instruction 'ring me' on it, so he did. The noise the bell made was unlike any other bell sound he had ever heard. He saw a shadow through the opaque window then the door was opened by a man in overalls. As soon as the man saw Harry he turned his head and shouted down the hallway, "It's all right, it ain't him," then turning back to Harry simply said, "Yes?" in an enquiring tone.

The lady of the house, still in her dressing gown came along the passage from the back of the house saying, "OK I'll sort it," to the man who had opened the door then squeezed out past Harry and checked up and down the road before turning and chivvying Harry inside, "Come about a room have you? Well come in then, don't just stand there," and Harry found himself in the hallway. He followed the lady up the stairs treading three or four steps behind her to look at the room. Sometimes he found life was like that, events were taken out of his hands and assumptions were made. Harry let it just happen, after all it was much easier to ride with the flow and he didn't have to take the room if he didn't like it.

The room was pleasant enough, clean and tidy and even had a sink in the corner of the room. Harry paid for a single night stay with the option of staying longer if needed. The woman, Sal, told Harry breakfast was at nine-ish and that if he wanted an evening meal, she could do one for him but of course that would be extra. Harry said no to the offer of the meal then took the room key and front door key proffered by Sal who had a final quick look around the room then said, "Don't forget, if you have any problems don't come to me," waited a brief moment for a response and when there wasn't one simply turned from the room and went downstairs.

Harry waited until she had finished thumping downstairs then put his suitcase on the bed and opened it to view its sparse contents. He hung his coat in the standing wardrobe, put his pyjamas under the pillow and turned back the duvet as his mother had always done, put his slippers under the bed, put his toiletry bag near the mandatory drink tray with kettle, cup and saucer and assortment of tea bags and coffee tubes, put the picture of Tyler on the mantelpiece over the boarded up fireplace and was left with Johnny Bunny and his old front door keys in the suitcase. Harry picked Johnny up briefly staring into nothingness as his hand kneaded the toy then put him back in the case which he put in the bottom of the wardrobe.

Not much for over thirty years of life he thought as he looked around the room at the brown linoleum floor and threadbare carpet and realized his life was full of negatives, no family, no friends, no roots. It was the first time that he began to think about his life and its' starkness struck him deeply.

He thought about the places he had stayed at over the years. Being a nomad had helped him to avoid relationships and settling too long in one place, but now faint stirrings of doubt about this kind of lifestyle began to rise.

***

1995

There were a lot of people attending the funeral of his parents but apart from a few school friends and their families, some teachers and neighbours, he did not know anyone there. His care worker had driven him there but he found her extremely irritating and did his best to get from under her too protective wings. He walked amongst the people for a while but felt their eyes on him as he went past them, which made him feel very awkward. The day was extremely cold and people had dressed up warm to combat it. Steam rose from their mouths as they talked to each other, so much so that from a distance, they looked like a human rain forest.

Harry looked over the flowers that had been laid out on one side of the pathway leading up to the church thinking that his Mum would not have liked them at all. She used to buy the dying, forgotten plants from garden shops and somehow always managed to revive them. Harry could remember standing in the kitchen doorway beside his Dad watching her talk and sing to them and they thrived. When his Mum caught 'her boys' watching her she would smile then make them a cup of tea and produce a plate of biscuits. Harry was lost in his reverie and was not aware that the hearses had arrived until his care worker touched him lightly on his upper arm and whispered in his ear.

Harry found himself sitting at the front of the church listening to someone who didn't know anything at all about his parents talk about them. He had had very little to do with how the service went although he did include one of his parents' favourite songs. It was not really appropriate for a funeral but it was played.

Harry listened, a huge lump in his throat. He guessed that people were waiting for him to cry but he was determined he wouldn't. Halfway through the song he had requested he suddenly got up from his seat and walked down the central aisle careful to avoid eye contact with anyone and out of the church then took a shuddering deep breath to calm himself. He wondered again at the number of people attending the funeral and supposed that funerals were a bit like weddings, people liked to go to them!

He leaned back against the side of the car that his care worker had brought him in and waited for her to come out. He thrust his chilled hands deep into his trouser pockets after turning up his collar and stamped his feet on the ground to try and engender some warmth in them.

His care worker was one of the first people to come out of the church after the service. He saw her looking around for him but gave no indication he had seen her. She stopped in front of him with a concerned look on her face asking him if he was all right but he just shrugged and stood back from the car so she could open it then sat in the back seat, pulled a baseball cap out of his pocket and put it on in such a way that his face was hidden.

His care worker started the car and waited a few minutes for the heater to breathe out warm air. She looked at Harry through the interior mirror, hunkered down in the back seat as he was then sighed and drove back to the residential home.

***

2019

Harry woke up in pitch blackness wondering for a moment where he was. He felt along the bed and managed to discover the bed lamp fixed as it was to the headboard and pulled the chord. The sudden brightness dazzled him for a moment and he blinked his eyes a few times to get used to it.

Harry was surprised at himself for falling asleep and thought that although he was still only in his thirties, he must be getting old. This was the first time that he could remember that he had fallen asleep during the day. Another indication that he was getting old he thought.

In the bathroom Harry washed the sleep out of his eyes then took a good look at himself in the bathroom mirror. While it was evident to him that he was no longer a teenager he didn't think he looked too bad, after all, how was thirty something supposed to look!

He dried his face off on the towel and returned it to his room then glanced at his watch and saw that it was only four thirty. Although he had no idea of what time it had been when he arrived, he thought that he had only been asleep for an hour or so, the pub lunch and the beer being the culprits.

Glancing out of the window to see if was raining or not Harry picked up his room keys and set off to the explore his surroundings, making sure he took note of the name of the road as only the number was written on the key tag.

The road he was in came out at the end of a High Street with few shops to start with and was mainly made up of dental practices, motels and residential houses.

Harry stopped to look in an estate agents window then found himself impulsively going inside to get an idea of the value of properties. He came out half an hour later totally shocked. The house he had lived in with his parents had been sold off along with artefacts, the money being put in trust for him when he was of age. He hadn't really touched it so, with interest, it had accrued into a nice little sum. However, house prices had since rocketed, and he now realised that a little property with a bit of land might be well out of his reach, well it was around this area anyway.

There were still plenty of people about and Harry actually felt part of the crowd instead of always being disengaged and on the outskirts. He was amazed to see some Christmas decorations up in some of the shops, where on earth had this year gone! He followed a group of adults into a large department store and looked around. He found a huge plate sized magnifying glass which reminded him of when he was a child and crawling around on his hands and knees in the back garden or in the local park with his Dad looking through microscopes to discover insects, then, on returning home, checking up in various books to see what they had discovered and making notes. He had had a fascination with ants and loved the way they organized themselves. Standing there with the huge magnifying glass had brought it all back to him and he was able to smile at the warm memories.

***

1998

Harry was being encouraged to enrol on a college course or find work, but his enthusiasm for either choice was at rock bottom.

He had been supported since his parents' untimely deaths, and had seen countless people who had tried to get him to open up but, since the day of the funeral when Harry had forced himself not to cry, not to show emotion, he now couldn't.

One of the real reasons that he didn't talk about his feelings was because he wanted to keep his private life just that, private. The thoughts were his and his alone and he was not going to share them with anybody. After a time though he realised that he would have to say something as he would never escape from the system that he found cloying. He started to give them what he thought they wanted and they did finally leave him alone.

Harry remembered returning to his parents' home with his care worker and another person who he now couldn't put a face or name to collect a few of his belongings shortly before the funeral took place. He hadn't wanted them to come inside the house as he felt it was an intrusion, but despite his protests they came inside anyway. The house felt different although it was still exactly as it was the last time the family had left it. He wanted to both take it all with him and, at the same time, leave it as it was. He went up to what had been his bedroom and pulled out and emptied an old brown suitcase that had once belonged to his grandad, although he had never seen him his Dad had talked about him with pride. He put items of clothing and some books in the case and was preparing to close it when he saw Johnny Bunny on the floor. He buried his head into the bunny and sobbed.

About an hour later he came downstairs with his suitcase which included a very wet Johnny Bunny. It was obvious that he had been crying but he was given space, he couldn't have been able to cope at that particular time if he had been shown sympathy.

He was the last one out of the house and closed the door behind him on that part of his life.

Harry finally enrolled in a drama class as he hadn't wanted to enrol in any of the other classes and the drama class was the remaining option.

The class was arranged in a circle of chairs and each person was given the opportunity to introduce themselves or 'pass' to the next person.

The class tutor was a stringy looking sort of chap who waved his arms around a lot as he spoke enthusiastically to them. They were given a timetable for the coming term and a list of books to study.

Harry couldn't understand what there was to study and felt just a bit uneasy about the choice he had made. Still, there was no going back, he would have to make the best of it.

Despite himself and his unease Harry realised that he had made a good choice. From sparse attendance at the beginning of term and dire warnings about being thrown (metaphorically) off of the course Harry was hooked in spite of himself. He had no trouble learning and remembering lines and enjoyed the visits out to different types of theatre and fell in love with an open theatre on the coast in Cornwall. He imagined himself acting there and felt really excited about such a prospect.

He was still able to attend the boxing lessons that had helped him curb or express his emotions over the years since the death of his parents and on the days when he didn't need to go into college he had the opportunity to develop his boxing skill, so all in all he felt he had his life sorted.

The class teacher, he found, was inspiring when you got to know him. He had watched the teacher performing a solo act and began to realise that there was more to acting than just acting.

The class went backstage to many theatres and rubbed shoulders with both beginners and famous actors. They watched live performances backstage seeing the differences between on stage and backstage performances.

The reputation of the drama class had previously been pretty bleak with live performances on campus to be avoided at all costs, but now students filled the drama studio enthusiastically. The end of course production was no exception, the studio was filled to the rafters so to speak.

Harry wandered onto the stage holding a microphone and waited for the noise to abate. It was discovered during the course of his ability to make an audience warm to him and to make them laugh, sometimes even without trying.

"Hello," he said. "My name is Smith, what's yours?"

The studio erupted again with people calling out their names but finally quietened as Harry patted an invisible dog.

Harry continued, "When I said Smith, that's my last name not my first, otherwise I would be called Smith Smith."

The studio audience erupted again but quietened quickly as Harry continued to talk to them.

"What do you call a fly without wings?" small pause "a walk."

"There's no point in getting a vacuum you'll be pleased to know, it just sits around gathering dust, a bit like some students I know!"

"I won't say our dog was lazy but my wife had to dust him off every day.

"We were very poor when we grew up, very, very poor but we did have a dishwasher, it was called Mum."

With the audience nicely warmed up Harry left the stage and got ready for his part in the performance.

The cast were brilliant and the team took bow after bow and, when it had all quietened down, they had a few celebratory drinks and food backstage before throwing their arms around one another exchanging numbers and good wishes.

Harry was one of the last to leave, he first of all shook hands with the tutor but then gave him a man hug. He really respected and liked the guy and was going to miss him. The tutor responded with, "Don't be a stranger," before turning away to talk to some of the few remaining students or their parents.

***

2019

Harry continued looking around the toy shop marvelling at the range available then bought himself a new shirt in the men's department before settling down to do some people watching whilst drinking a large cup of coffee. He had a second cup then decided to go for a walk to get to know the area.

He felt really relaxed and happy and even found himself whistling tunes that he had heard in some shops. He bought one of the left-over daily papers and a local one, rolled and tucked them under his arm and strolled off.

An hour or so later of meandering he found himself passing a public house and went inside and ordered himself a stone baked pizza with sides and a pint and settled down to read the papers. The local paper was a real community paper, gossipy but homely and Harry read it through, from back to front, getting a real feel for the ethos of the area. There was a big spread on the back page about the local football team with photographs, a section about the local beekeepers talking about swarms, school exam results, pudding recipes from the Mothers Union, yet another person missing on the moors, bring and buy sales, church jumble sales, photography courses at the local university, letters of complaint about anything and everything with the frontpage broadcasting in bold print 'child bites dog'.

There was a large screen in the public house showing a football match and although Harry was not bothered which of the teams would win, he enjoyed it immensely.

Picking up his newspapers he left the public house but instead of crossing the road and returning to his B & B he kept on the same side of the road and followed the road that cut through the moors.

After about a quarter of a mile he left the road and walked into the moors for a hundred yards or so, stopped suddenly and took deep satisfying breaths. Harry must have stood still for about five minutes or so but soon turned back to the road and returned to his lodgings feeling more at peace than he had in a long time.

Once in his room he threw the papers on the bed, washed and changed into his pyjamas then settled in bed and reached for the daily paper, only really looking at headlines as he thumbed through it. He didn't find anything to grab his attention but thumbed back through it in case there was anything interesting before he turned out the light.

An unusual surname caught his eye in an article about a middle-aged mother, Renate, who had tried for years to have a child paying out thousands of pounds before finally giving up then falling pregnant naturally three years ago and had now found out she was pregnant again. Harry read through the story again and again taking in the image of the 'happy family'.

Harry stared into the distance for a moment then got up from the bed and strode around the room getting more and more agitated 'It can't be', he thought, 'it can't be, no, not after all this time.' He picked up the paper and read the article again and then again. The more he read it the more certain he became that he was right, the husband of Renate was the man who had been at the wheel of the 4 x 4 that had decimated his parents, he was sure of it.

His brain zigzagged between extremes of certainty and uncertainty.

The article had opened up a floodgate and he was finding it difficult to deal with thoughts and emotions that he thought had been dealt with all those years ago.

It was the boxing more than anything else that had helped him to cope with and live with himself after his parents had died, after all he blamed himself for their death and no matter what anyone said to him he reasoned that if his parents had not gone to the shopping centre that day to buy him a birthday present they would still be here!

The strict regime of training taught him more about himself than countless years of therapy had, or so he thought at the time. In the ring the desire to take out his aggression on somebody else continually found him knocked to the floor and although he kept getting up to renew his attack he still got defeated. He didn't listen to the coach or anybody, he was at the age when he knew best, and it wouldn't change until he realized that the advice he was given was for his benefit and not given to him just for the sake of it.

Harry did learn and, in the end, became quite a good boxer winning a few titles in his youth. Yes, he was certain that without the boxing or the drama course he wouldn't have kept sane.

Now he didn't know what to think, he tossed and turned in the bed most of the night finally falling asleep during the early hours of the morning and thankfully his nightmares left him alone.

After his breakfast Harry paid in advance for another night then left for the library taking yesterday's newspaper with him and buying a notepad and pencil from the newsagents.

Harry had a very difficult day in the library staring at the headlines of the day and there it was, in black and white, the strange surname that had hooked his attention. The driver of the 4 x 4 had suffered a heart attack and had undergone surgery upon reaching the hospital. The report stated that he was lucky to be alive given the severity of the accident.

Harry wanted to see the man, in the flesh, and find out if he was the driver from all those years ago. He didn't know what he was going to say or do, he just knew, he had to see him. He tried to use common sense and talk himself out of it but all he managed to do was talk himself into it.

He had spent so long in the library that he had forgotten to eat but now his stomach was reminding him that it needed filling. He rubbed a hand over his face and blinked several times to try to normalize his eyes which were tired from staring at the computer screen, then put his notepads and pencil in his pocket and left the library.

It was a pleasant early evening with quite a lot of people milling around. Harry went in to the first public house on his route back to the B & B and ordered a meal and a pint. There was a lovely atmosphere in the pub with a live band called the 'Blue Mantis' playing in the rear room. The music was lively and Harry enjoyed listening to it as he waited for his meal. He began to relax finally for the first time that day but when he started to fall asleep, he deemed it was time to go, so he did.

***

2009

Harry managed to get himself a job as a compere in a holiday hotel and found the job very much to his liking. The deal included a nominal rent flat and his food so he considered himself lucky.

He became friendly with one of the chefs who also had accommodation in the hotel. The chef owned a white Samoyed dog and Harry spent many hours with 'Tyler' taking him for long runs/walks in the park when his owner was working, playing games with him, grooming his beautiful white coat or simply lounging with him. Tyler was a great lounger, a typical teenager in dog guise.

On one of the walks with Tyler Harry suddenly sat on one of the park benches and poured his heart out to Tyler who sat in front of him staring up into his face. He told Tyler everything over the course of months of park walks and Tyler either put a paw up onto his knee, tilted his head sideways or did both, knowing perhaps that he looked incredibly cute.

Harry did not know if he was happy or not, the only time he had feelings of any sort he could relate to was when he was out with Tyler, and Tyler was good at keeping his secrets, bless him.

Pet therapy was awesome.

The job paid reasonably good money so Harry did not have to dip into his bank account, all in all he was fairly well settled. During the evening he found out which acts were on, what they entailed, how long they would last and the sequence they would appear. He enjoyed the job and was thankful for his experiences in the drama class which enabled him to project an image to the audience whilst at the same time keeping himself private.

During one evening one of the acts was taken sick moments before their appearance and it was part of Harrys' contract to fill in.

Harry introduced himself as the compere, walked off of the stage, took his jacket off and slung it around his shoulders, scruffed up his hair then walked onto the stage and threw his arms out wide to acknowledge the applause. His "cloak" fell off from around his shoulders and as he turned to pick it up, he tripped over his deliberately undone shoelaces.

The jokes came thick and fast and left the audience, metaphorically, in stitches.

"I got on a bus the other day, you know, those big red things that come along in twos and threes, and sat on the only seat available at the front, you know, those reserved for pregnant women or the disabled. Well anyway the voice of a bloke sitting at the back of the bus came over crystal clear. He had obviously hurt his leg as he had on one of those strap-on boot things and was holding onto a crutch with one hand whilst he was holding the mobile he was shouting into with the other. Do you know what he said, he said "Someone has just got onto the bus (me) and I can't tell whether it's a bloke or a bird." Crystal clear. Well, you have to laugh don't you, there was this bloke one the bus having a go about me and he was sitting there loud as life holding on to his crutch. I ask you!"

He was a master of innuendo and had quite a following and would, perhaps, have stayed longer in the job if his friend the chef, hadn't had to leave due to family circumstances. He missed his friend but he missed Tyler even more and, in the end, he left the job and returned to being a nomad.

***

2019

Harry left for London on an early morning train after paying rent a week in advance. He had no idea of why he wanted to come back to the area, he just went with his gut feeling.

He arrived in London mid-morning and checking he had the correct address, he set off. There were crowds of people bustling about of many nationalities, which Harry loved as he thought diversity broadened the mind.

Arriving at the address Harry went inside and explained to the private eye what he wanted, gave his name and current address, paid up front, shook hands then left.

Harry found himself on Albert Bridge, which was one of his favourite bridges, and stopped and watched the waterway traffic on the muddy coloured Thames.

He treated himself to a ride on the London Eye then went for a stroll along the Embankment, stopping for a meal on one of the floating restaurants moored alongside it. He loved London he realised, it was just brilliant. He was a big fan of graffiti, but only the good kind and saw enough to keep him sated for the rest of his life.

His train ride back was uneventful and he arrived early enough to call in to the public house he had visited on the first day he arrived. He took his drink out back and stood looking out over the moors, feeling strange that he was so drawn to them.

Over the next couple of days, he explored the area and discovered quite a few craft shops tucked away in side streets. He was becoming comfortable with the area but this did not trigger the urge to travel to a different place as it would normally have done. He knew what he wanted to do with his life now and was content to see how that would pan out. Ever since he had seen the young baby on the train, he had wondered what his own children would look like. He knew he was getting ahead of himself but at last he was beginning to have direction, to have purpose.

Two days later a large envelope was delivered for him. He left it unopened whilst he finished his breakfast then took it to read in the local park.

Harry sat on a bench by the lake and watched people rowing boats and the ducks and swans seemingly swimming effortlessly by leaving v-shaped troughs in their wake, leaving the envelope unopened on the bench beside him. He thought about the events that had brought him to this moment in time, the fact that he had bought a newspaper with that article inside it when he hadn't bought a newspaper for years. He didn't know if it was karma or just chance or fate, but decided he would just go along for the ride with whatever it was.

He rolled the thoughts around in his mind and decided that whatever it was, he needed to open the envelope.

Harry opened it and carefully read through the contents a few times. Satisfied with the content he returned everything back in the envelope then sat and let the information mull through his brain.

He had thought to leave his journey until the following day but on impulse went to the station, checked out the route and changes he would have to make then boarded the train. He was both excited and scared or was it scared and excited! Anyway, he was on his way with no idea of what he was going to say or do but one thing was sure, he was finally going to find the man who had killed his parents.

The train journey seemed to take no time at all including waiting for connections, but within three hours he was nearly at his destination.

The tree-lined road seemed very pleasant and the autumn colours of the leaves made it more so.

He walked along the road checking the numbers or names of the houses as he went. Most of the houses were double bay and although he tried hard not to form assumptions Harry reckoned that the family must be doing well for themselves if they were still able to live in such an area, even after spending so much trying to have a child.

Harry was so intent on checking the numbers of the houses that he didn't notice somebody backing out of a car whilst at the same time trying to pull something heavy from the passenger seat. The heavy article seemed to offer resistance but instead of going around to the passenger door and collecting it from there the man had thought that he could do it the hard way. One final jerk and the article was free taking him by surprise and he staggered backwards knocking into Harry, both of them falling in a tangled heap on the pavement with Harry trapped underneath and knocking his head on the garden wall.

"I'm so terribly sorry," the man said scrambling off of Harry then bent over him to check he was all right staring into his face. "Are you all right? I don't know what I was thinking. Are you sure you're not hurt?" Harry blinked his eyes rapidly a few times then stared into the face hovering a few inches in front of him. He noticed that there was jagged scaring on the right side of the mans' face which had drawn up his mouth making it lopsided. Harry reassured him that he was fine, just fine, holding both hands up to his chest, to show that he was.

"Daddy, Daddy!" called a young child who was making her way down the path of the house they were in front of accompanied by a yappy little dog, "Daddy I'm coming." In the doorway, watching the child, stood a heavily pregnant lady who called out to the child to be careful but neither the child or the dog took any notice as they got in the way of each other going down the path towards the front gate.

Harry recognised the woman from the newspaper picture and realized that the man who had spoken to him was the man in the picture. The man who had killed his parents. This realization seemed to make time stand still as he stared into the man's face for what seemed like a lifetime. He could see the man's lips moving as he spoke to him but could not hear anything at all. Harry felt light headed and swayed on his feet.

The young child reached the gate and lifted up her arms whilst calling out to her daddy but the man was looking at Harry, his face full of concern. Somehow Harry found himself walking up the garden path towards the house whilst the yappy dog squirmed around his ankles with delight, its tail going nineteen to the dozen. The man, who had picked up his daughter to carry her back to the house followed Harry along the path and settled him onto the settee in the front room whilst explaining to his wife that he had accidentally backed into Harry and had knocked him over whilst backing out of the car. His wife smiled fondly at him, telling him he was getting too lazy in his old age to walk around to the other side of the car, then busied herself making tea.

The yappy dog jumped up on Harry's lap and tried to wash him whilst little Moreen giggled with glee, her hands clasped with delight in front of her.

The family were delightful, so obviously caring for each other and for him also. Two cups of tea and a plate of biscuits later, taken mostly by cute little Moreen who then fed them to the dog, Harry was finally able to make his excuses and leave.

Whatever he had expected Harry hadn't expected what had happened to happen. He didn't know what to think apart from the fact that he had liked them very much.

To his surprise, it was much earlier than he had thought so he took the central line across London then, a short bus ride to the cemetery, where his parents were buried. His nomadic lifestyle meant that he didn't visit as often as he would have liked but he knew that he had to come, today was a special day and he needed to talk to them. Harry bought a pot plant from the flower shop near the cemetery and went inside and walked unerringly to the plot where his parents were buried.

After the funeral Harry had resisted all efforts to visit the cemetery saying why would anybody want him to visit the partial remains of his parents. Within a few years this changed and he became a regular visitor needing the solace of being near his parents. He found that he could talk to them for hours if need be, and often did.

Harry narrated one of the war poems that his parents had been so fond of, learning it by rote until he knew it backwards and forwards and inside out, then planted the pot plant making sure that the roots were free as his Mum had shown him.

Harry decided it was too late to travel back so he booked a room in the Premier Inn and spent time sorting his head out. He had tried not to have any expectations when meeting the man and his family who had caused him such trauma in his life but he hadn't thought that he would actually like and get along with them.

Lots of things he couldn't yet put a name to were changing in him and he recognised that he had made a momentous leap forward today. Talking to his parents had enabled him to get some structure in his thinking.

He could hear his Dad saying, "Everything happens for a reason even if we don't know or ever know the reason." Harry now found this to be a truth whereas he had once scoffed at the idea.

His sleep was restful and the following morning he was relaxed and happy with himself. He was beginning to accept himself and like himself as he was, warts and all.

Harry visited the cemetery again during the morning then started on his return journey to the B & B. The journey back was uneventful but Harry thought he would lay down for an hour or two when he got back to the B & B as he felt jaded. On passing the The Swalk, he noticed a chalked sign advertising live music that evening and decided, as he crossed over the road from it, that he would go there later that evening.

Once in his room Harry stretched out on the bed and soon fell fast asleep.

***

The Swalk

Harry had decided that the following day would be spent in the library looking at prices of properties, preferably not too far from the coast, in different parts of the country. He had no idea where he would end up living but he found the prospect exciting and not at all daunting. He would go where the wind blew him or, in other words, end up somewhere by chance. He would use the skills acquired by his nomad lifestyle to find a place he could settle in. He smiled at the irony of the thought.

    Harry woke up early evening feeling refreshed and raring to go. He tidied himself up then left the B & B and walked up the road at a jaunty pace, collar turned up and hands thrust deep in his pockets. He could hear the heartbeat of the music well before he reached the end of the road but when he reached the corner he almost needed dark glasses to counter the dazzling illuminations that battered his visual sense.

    The Swalk, it seemed, had spared no expense for the coming Christmas festivities and flashing lights and laser beams let everyone know that fact. Harry thought that the public house would not be out of place in Oxford Street. He thought it was well OTT but had to smile at the uplifting effect it seemed to have on everyone.

A large inflatable Father Christmas bobbed and weaved in time to the music, it seemed, parts of its 'anatomy' scribed with crude comments but some of which were really funny.

Her suddenly took a mental picture of himself standing outside a pub reading graffiti on a blow up of Father Christmas and he laughed out loud causing people nearby to look his way.

He was still laughing when he entered the pub and pushed his way to the bar and bought himself a local brew and ordered a stone-based pizza. Harry managed to find an unoccupied stool with a reasonably clear view of the band and settled himself, his feet tapping against the stool rungs.

The band, The Blue Mantis, were the same band he had heard a few days previously in a public house across town, and although some of the music had changed since he was a youth there was still room for some good old rock and roll.

When his pizza arrived, he had to vacate the stool as he had found it impossible to eat it and hold onto his drink at the same time. He went out of the back door of the pub into the seated area and found himself a bench seat and ate his meal with relish, sharing some of it with a cheeky fox that had hopped over the wall separating the area from the moors, not at all put out by the illuminations, crowds, or noise. Harry watched it for a while awed by its' beauty and when it disappeared back over the wall Harry got up and went to where the fox had jumped over but he could not see anything at first, cloaked in blackness as it was. He stayed for a while staring into the blackness and, as his eyes adjusted, he was able to make out some shapes, but of the fox there was nothing to be seen.

Harry went back inside suddenly feeling the chill of the night and found himself pulled onto the dance floor. He copied some of the modern gyrations with difficulty and then found someone who could do some old-fashioned rock and roll and really excelled himself, earning a round of applause for both himself and his partner. At the end of the dance, which had taken more out of him than he cared to admit, he decided he needed another drink and asked his 'partner' if she would like one also. Just as she was about to reply a man appeared alongside her and pulled her away so that answered that.

Harry was really enjoying himself and felt part of the crowd. He wasn't lonely or doing peripheral surfing, he was right in the thick of things and loving every minute.

Whilst at the bar he found himself alongside one of the band members and, on impulse, bought him a drink. They got chatting, exchanged names, Martin was his name, shook hands then talked music till it was time for Martin to return back onto the stage.

The time flew passed and whisked away the rest of the day and all to soon Harry found himself out of the pub and waiting for his turn to share a permanent marker to write a comment on the Father Christmas. It wasn't as easy to do as it had looked as the Father Christmas either blew into him, smothering him or away from him so he was having to chase it.

He managed to write a fairly illegible soliloquy, giggling to himself as he wrote it then passed the pen onto someone else and suddenly turned and walked away from the group and around the side of The Swalk onto the moors.

He had no idea how long he had walked but it must have been a fair time as he could not see the lurid lights of the public house or hear anything at all for that matter.

Just himself and the moor but Harry was not at all daunted, in fact he felt more at peace than he had in a long, long time. He breathed in deeply the chill night air and let it out slowly before turning back. After only a few short steps he suddenly fell to his knees on the chilled earth and cried as he had not allowed himself to do since his parents had died. Great shuddering sobs racked his body as he cried long and loud, his head thrown back, his mouth wide open. The tears he couldn't or wouldn't allow himself to cry flowed easily releasing years of pent up anguish, pain and loneliness.

Harry did not have any idea how long he cried but as the shuddering sobs eased, he felt as if a great burden had been lifted off of him. He got to his knees, brushing down his damp knees then straightened up, 'Harry' he thought 'this is the beginning of the rest of your life,' and emboldened by that thought he strode back the way he had come brushing the tears from beneath his eyes whilst, at the same time, adding a smudge of damp moorland across his cheeks.

***

Performance

Harry found himself waiting in the wings of a place he didn't recognise watching a balancing act. The audience seemed very responsive and their applause and laughter echoed around the building. He didn't remember taking this booking but the compere, who looked vaguely familiar, seemed to know him well and expected him so he supposed he must be in the right place, wherever it was.

The balancing act drew to a close and the compere walked briskly onto the stage as they came off and began his build-up of Harry, then threw his left arm out towards Harry encouraging him to make his entrance which he did with alacrity throwing his arms wide so that his cloak (undone around his shoulders) fell off and tripping over his purposely undone shoe laces when he bent to retrieve it. He sat down on the stage with his legs straight out in front of him and did up his shoe laces, "Right over left, twist under, make a loop etc." That done he made an effort to get up but found it very difficult as he had a horrible pain in his left hip and couldn't feel his left leg.

As Harry rolled around the floor trying to get up the audience was in stitches and clapped and whistled thinking this was part of his act. He eventually managed to stand as numbness replaced the pain and found himself facing the curtain 'Now where have you all gone?' whilst peering around and under the curtain then suddenly turning around towards the audience he jumped as if shocked to see them then, taking the microphone off of its' stand he began his routine…

"My Mum bought a vacuum cleaner, you know, one of those things that just sits around gathering dust. Waste of money if you ask me, all of a sudden, the dog's not good enough. Anyway, it came with a lot of bits that you can never find when you want them and one of these bits was called a crevice tool. Seriously. Now what springs to mind when you think of a crevice tool, certainly not a spare part of a vacuum cleaner that's for sure."

"I went into my local shop yesterday and they told me nothing was ready so I said that's all right, I'll have a packet of nothing, no no, whilst I'm here make it two packets."

"Does anyone know where the toilet is?" Harry asked suddenly feeling a desperate need of one as he leant forwards from the hip whilst pulling a face that would have won him first place in a gurning competition. "Do you know" he said, suddenly standing upright, "I like you."

The audience clapped and cheered, whistled, and stamped their feet in response.

"Isn't it funny how we name things. Mum got a lovely big German shepherd dog, thinking it would get me up off of my backside to take it for walks. It was a cracking dog and to tell the truth we were lucky to get him as he had previously been a guard dog in a public house but had been thrown out after he ate drugged meat and had slept all the way through a raid. The pub landlord literally gave him away. Unbelievable."

"Anyway, getting back to the point, the dog's name was Donut but I never called him that when we were out. You start yelling 'Donut', where I live, and you'll end up with a fat lip."

"My mate's dog thinks that it is called 'F..k off'.

The audience continued to stamp and whistle and Harry suddenly thought that they were not really listening to him and that they would continue to be loud and noisy whatever he said. Still, he thought, he would make the most of their apparent appreciation as who was to say when he would perform again!

"My Mum calls me fortnight, amongst other things. She thinks that I am too weak to do anything."

"My Mum got an insect bite on her face the other day and it came up something awful. I offered to go with her to the walk-in clinic (put a blanket over her head like) but she said not to bother as it was cheaper than botox."

"Here," he said leaning conspiratorially forward and glancing meaningfully both ways "this one is for the fellas. I know some of you have your wife sitting next to you but don't worry, she ain't listening. He glanced both ways again and leaned even further forward, "Does your wife say things to you, you don't understand and you don't know whether she's doing it on purpose or being funny?" He stood up and nodded to himself. "My wife calls me a regular guy, what does she mean by that? Is it as insulting as calling me trustworthy and reliable? Do you think she really means I'm boring." He held his arms out to the audience, palms turned upward then leaned forward again and cupped his mouth with one hand. "Her nickname for me is tampon. Yes, you heard it right, tampon. Well, I'm not having that, what does she think I am, stupid. I confronted her and asked her straight out – regular or super plus."

Harry stood up and rubbed a hand across his forehead and found he was sweating profusely. He felt light-headed and giddy and had to hold on to the stand-up microphone. The audience thought it was part of his act and continued to laugh and wolf whistle. The pain in his hip came back with a vengeance and he turned to the compere, who was watching him with concern, and signalled to bring on a chair for him. He had an act to finish and by heaven he was going to finish it. He sent a mental message out to his parents asking them to help him and provide enough energy for him to finish his act and almost immediately felt better. He sat on the chair and told the audience that his view was better than theirs.

The atmosphere was warm and electric. Harry loved the crowd and thought that he would come here again when he found out where he was. The thought made him laugh, he was performing and he had no idea where the place was!

"I wish that I could take you with me wherever I go, you are simply amazing," Harry told them from the heart.

"My Mum said that she didn't want me to buy her a Christmas present this year, 'just turn up' she said. I should have left it there but of course I didn't. I kept on at her and the last time I said it I was going to agree and say all right, I'll just bring myself but she suddenly said "Oh go on then, I want a Vegan telly". Well, I tell you, they are very rare, I haven't been able to discover one anywhere so I am going to be in big trouble."

"Oh, by the way, did I tell you that all the money from this event is going to The Brooke charity!" It's written there in your programme on the inside of the first page in case you haven't noticed it yet so I want to thank all of you from the bottom of my heart."

Harry caught sight of the compere in the wings who signalled to him that he only had a short time left. He was both surprised and amazed, where on earth had the time gone, it felt like he had only just started.

"My girlfriend suddenly started giving me a hard time. It would have been all right if it was the other way round, but it wasn't. She said that if I didn't want to get married, I should get out of her life, I ask you. How unfair is that! We've been going out for such a short time, coming up to twelve years, but anyway I bowed to pressure and told her February 30th!"

"What's big and yellow and eats rocks… A big yellow rock eater!"

Harry suddenly slumped in his seat. The audience thought that it was part of his act but after a few minutes the compere and a stage hand came on and carefully carried Harry off into the wings. The compere then returned on to the stage and told the quietened audience that Harry was receiving medical attention but would appreciate one final round of applause. The audience responded louder than ever for a few minutes then gradually began to disperse.

Harry sat slumped in the chair, he couldn't understand why he felt so drained. Suddenly he roused himself, 'surely not' he thought to himself, that sounds like Mum and Dad, I never saw them in the audience. He opened his weary eyes and looked around and suddenly caught sight of them, they were here, they were really here. There were tears in his eyes as he got up with great difficulty and staggered towards them his arms wide. The three met and fell into each others' arms, supporting each other in a triangle shape, with Harry saying, "Mum, Dad, I've missed you so much, I love you, I love you."

***

The Moor

Harry was not seen again by any living person although many of the wildlife inhabitants of the moors had come across him. As he was walking back from his outpouring of grief with a determination to live his life to the full from now on his right leg stepped in to a hidden narrow fissure and his body, propelled forward by momentum crashed into the narrowing length of the fissure which fitted him perfectly, lengthwise at least, like a coffin with vegetation, when it recovered from the intrusion, for a lid.

Harry had felt a brief sense of fear from his chest area as he had stepped into nothingness but was mercifully knocked unconscious as his upper body laid him to rest in a position that he would remain in until his body decayed sufficiently to allow it to slip down and eventually drop, piece by piece, into the void beneath him, thereby joining up with literally hundreds, perhaps thousands, of human and animal remains.

Harry was wedged lying mostly on his right side with his face angled down into the fissure, his heavy unconscious body assimilating into the shape of the surrounding area. Harrys' left leg had almost been ripped from his body and had come to rest at a peculiar angle aside from facing the other way, not that anyone would ever know.

Mercifully he did not know what had happened or what was happening to him. His eyes, wide open, were staring down into the blackness of the void. He didn't see the darkness, however, he saw with the utmost clarity the stage and the audience to whom he was performing.

As his life slipped away, he was in his glory having just given the performance of his life in front of a packed audience. His lips were moving almost imperceptibly and issued the tiniest of sounds as he poured out the jokes which had come thick and fast as they had earlier in his life. He only had to open his mouth and the jokes poured out. His Mum had always called him her little comedian and he was, born and bred. He thanked God for giving him the chance to discover this ability within himself. Just as he fell into his parents arms his heart stopped beating, his lips stopped moving but his blood continued, for a little while longer, to drain into his surroundings and drip into the void below.

***

Tyler

Tyler was restless and walked up and down the hallway and kitchen, his nails clicking on the tiled surface. His owner, the chef, was out at work although he was due in any moment. Tyler stopped briefly by the back door peering out past his reflection into the blackness beyond then continued his pacing making little sounds of distress. Halfway through pacing the hallway, he suddenly stopped, raised his head into the classic wolf pose and howled.

When the chef arrived home, he chatted to Tyler as usual, put on the radio for some background noise and made himself a cup of tea. When the tea had cooled sufficiently, he poured some into Tyler's bowl but when this didn't engender a response, he put his mug of tea on the floor and sat down by Tyler's bed.

Tyler hadn't moved at all since his owner had returned home laying in his bed as he was with his paws covering his muzzle. The chef stroked him gently between his ears and talked gently to him but still Tyler didn't move.

When the chef said, "What's the matter old chap, have you lost someone?" Tyler put his head up and stared into his face. "Whoever you have lost, I am sure they are now in a better place," he said giving Tyler one last hug before getting up and getting on with preparing himself for bed as he had an early shift in the morning.

The chef let Tyler out into the garden to make himself comfortable before going to bed. Tyler sat down in the middle of the lawn and howled, his mournful song drifting up into the black sky.

***

Sal

The following day Sal, the landlady, knocked on the door of the room she had let to Harry and, when there was no reply, opened the door and went in. The room was spotless Sal noticed as she stood in the middle of it and looked around. The bed was neatly turned down with his pyjamas folded and placed beneath the pillow, the slippers placed neatly side by side under the bed. She hadn't heard Harry come in the previous night and it was hard to tell whether he had come in with the room being so neat and tidy.

His room had been paid up until this morning and, with the possessions still in the room it was possible that Harry would stay longer. She hoped so as tenants were hard to come by this time of year and he seemed such a nice young man.

Sal roused herself from her daydreaming and left the room quickly and went downstairs. Although it was her house she didn't want to be deemed to have been prying in the room if Harry came back suddenly, she would wait and see what tomorrow would bring.

The following day Sal came back into the room and saw that everything still looked untouched. She opened the wardrobe door and found the battered brown suitcase which she took out and put on the bed. Picking up the pyjamas from under the pillow she opened the case and found Johnny bunny, worn and threadbare but obviously much loved and a set of keys with a picture of two people she did not know, his parents perhaps she thought. Sal was surprised that a young man would carry around a childhood comforter but then what did she know, she had hung onto lots of things from her now grown-up children and wouldn't part with them or the memories they invoked. She picked up Johnny bunny and thought, 'That's it, it's not so much the object, it's more the memories attached to them.' She put Johnny kindly back into the suitcase, packed the pyjamas and slippers into it then walked around the room to see if there was anything else to pack away. She found a picture of Tyler on the mantlepiece and on picking it up she turned it over and read 'Tyler' on the back of it. She looked at the picture of the Samoyed dog and put it in her pocket instead of the suitcase, found a bag of wash stuff in one of the top drawers of the chest of drawers, put it into the suitcase and took it downstairs where it ended up in the cupboard under the stairs until the young man came to collect it. If he didn't Sal thought, she would have to think what to do with it but enough of that for now, she could do with a nice hot cup of tea.

Sal sat down at the kitchen table to drink her tea and took the picture of Tyler out of her pocket. She had never seen such a beautiful dog before. Finishing her tea, she took the picture and wedged it in the corner of a large picture she had of galloping horses then made herself another cup of tea.

Over the years, Sal took the picture of Tyler down to look more closely at it and soon became convinced that Tyler was a dog she had known as a child, and that they had been inseparable!